TALES FROM THE OLD INN

To
Caroline

Regards
Jim Radley

And lots of love ♡
from Nicky .

TALES FROM THE OLD INN

TWO WYRD BARCHESTER STORIES

JIM RADLEY

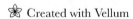

For Jemma
1965-2015

CONTENTS

PREFACE

"Footfall" is an original story for this volume. An earlier version of "Still Waters" was published on my blog.

PROLOGUE

A medieval cathedral city, let us call it Barchester, built on the confluence of five rivers, crisscrossed by ley lines, encircled by ancient monuments and secret government establishments. A place where the past lies very near the surface, and strange events are almost a daily occurrence.

FOOTFALL

BRIDGET'S STORY

FOOTFALL

The Talespinners had finished second in the final pub quiz before Christmas, losing by one point due to their ignorance of the latest romantic entanglements of the Jenner/Kardashian dynasty. Peter, the Librarian, said they should regard this as a badge of honour. The others agreed, up to a point, though the prize money would have been very welcome at this most wonderful, most expensive, time of the year.

The group of five, who always sat at the large round table to the left of the inglenook fireplace in The Old Inn, took their team name from another regular Sunday night ritual: that of spinning each other yarns relating to weird or unusual events they had experienced. By general agreement it was decreed that the stories must be "substantially" true. Slight embellishments were allowed to make the tales more satisfying in the telling, but the basic facts had to be genuine.

Since they all lived in Barchester, such embroidery was rarely necessary.

Since they all lived in Barchester, there was no shortage of stories to tell.

Mark, the Programmer, manoeuvred a tray of drinks to the table, and passed glasses round. A Guinness for himself, a G&T for Vivienne, and pints of golden New Forest ale for the other three.

"Your turn tonight," he said to Bridget as he handed her her pint.

Bridget was in her late fifties, with a strong face under an untidy bun of salt-and-pepper hair, in which was stuck the pencil she had used for her quiz answers. She was an archivist working for the cathedral, and the impression that she was a slightly scatty academic was understandable but profoundly mistaken.

Bridget waited until Mark had taken his seat before speaking.

"I'm not one for talking off the cuff," she began. The others tried to shout her down but she silenced them with a wave of her hand. "No, seriously. I've written this down, so I hope you don't mind if I read it out rather than attempting to improvise." The four other Talespinners agreed, took sips of their drinks, and settled back to listen. The roaring fire in the inglenook hearth crackled cosily, sleet splattered against the windowpanes and the hubbub of the Old Inn seemed to fade into the background.

"This happened in the mid-eighties, just after Christmas. I had recently moved on to the new Hill-side estate up near the hill fort. It was the first winter since it had been completed and many of the houses were still empty, but those of us living there had already formed a friendly community. My house – my first after moving out of my parents' place on the London Road – was a two-up, two-down shoebox, but most of the new buildings were three or four bedroom semis, and therefore attractive to young families."

Bridget took a sip of her ale before reading on.

They're called "desire paths" or sometimes "use paths", or, more prosaically "social paths". We pass examples every day, probably without even noticing them. One I think we'd all recognise is on Watermill Lane by Queen Mary Gardens: the pedestrian crossing doesn't line up with the paved path into the park, so over the years a short cut has been worn down, ten metres of trampled earth across the grass in a direct line between the crossing and the footpath. A canny planning department would incorporate the unofficial path, but don't get me started on that!

The residents on the new estate had noticed one of these paths had appeared on the steep slope between Hillside Avenue and Castle Lane, through the couple of acres of scrubby woodland the developers had left to help preserve the views from the hill fort. Quite what had prompted their complaints was unclear, but the fact was the homeowners didn't like the path. It seemed sinister and vaguely unpleasant. People reported that they, and more specifically their children, had been disturbed by it, or by somebody or something on it, and there were rumours of a flasher, or worse.

A rather strange thing was that there was a perfectly good tarmac footpath only a few yards away, on a gentle gradient and well lit. The desire path was neither, and in fact was quite significantly longer. There was no reason for it to be preferred to the official footpath.

The other strange thing about the desire path was that no one was ever seen to use it.

A couple of my neighbours discovered that I had connections with the City Council, and asked me if I could do anything. As I lived at the other end of the estate, and used my old Morris Minor to commute to work at the cathedral, I had been unaware of the existence of the path. I was unsure what I was supposed to do – there was talk of "blocking it off" – but I agreed to have a look anyway.

I arrived on a beautiful sunny afternoon two days after Christmas, bright but cold, with a few inches of crisp snow lying on the roads. It was the school holidays, obviously, and children were out with toboggans or trying to ride the skateboards or BMX bikes they had received as gifts. Computer games were still in their infancy at that time, and of course Facebook wasn't yet a twinkle in Mark Zuckerberg's eye, so kids really did play outside all day, even in winter.

The start of the desire path was easy enough to spot, a worn patch of well-trodden earth beside a lamppost on a curve in the road, close to the official footpath. The curve lay in a dip and was in shadow even on this bright morning. The first thing I noticed was that the path wasn't even straight. It wound sinuously out of sight as it went downhill under the darkness of the trees – a darkness which seemed deeper than the shadows you'd expect in a winter woodland. This was definitely not a commonplace example of an opportunistic short cut. Although snow blanketed the undergrowth, the path was completely clear, as though scores of feet had recently passed that way.

I stepped off the pavement.

Now, we're all native to Barchester and we all know what the city and the surrounding area can be like. We can all list places which have a weird "vibe" and

I'm sure I'm not the only one who outright refuses to set foot in certain spots. So when I tell you that I'd never felt such an intense reaction to a location as I did then, I hope you'll appreciate quite how serious I'm being.

As I said, it was a bright winter's day, and although chilly it was pleasant, but that one step off the pavement might as well have transported me beyond the Arctic Circle. I didn't just start shivering – my teeth began to chatter. The happy uproar and laughter of the playing kids disappeared, to be replaced with nothing but silence. The loudest noise was the thump of my pulse in my ears, and instantly my heart was racing.

I stuck it out for about a minute, though it seemed far longer. I backed up slowly, until I felt the soles of my boots touch concrete once more. The happy noise of the children at play suddenly returned, as if someone had switched from "Mute" to full volume. I realised I must have been holding my breath, and gasped for air. After being so chilled, I was now sweating.

Once I had recovered some of my equilibrium I walked back up the road towards the group of kids. They were aged, I'd say, between eight and thirteen, equal numbers of boys and girls. I suppose it shows how much things have changed in the years since, but I didn't have any hesitation in approaching them, nor did they seem to have any in talking to me.

"I'm from the council," I said to the oldest-looking boy, stretching the truth somewhat. "We're interested in finding out about that path there."

"What path?" he replied.

"Down on the corner. The path through the trees," I said.

Everyone went very quiet. The two youngest looking kids backed away. The bottom lip of one starting to tremble noticeably.

"We don't know nothing about that." the eldest boy said, defensively.

"Look, nobody's in any trouble. If you use it as a short cut, that's fine…" I began.

"We don't use it as a short cut."

"We don't go anywhere near it," added one of the girls, as if that was the end of the conversation, and she bundled the youngest kids away maternally.

I fixed the eldest boy with a stern look, daring him to keep eye contact. Although at the time I was only just out of my teens myself, it was enough of an age gap to give me authority.

"Tell me what you know," I said.

He looked uncertain for a while, then said "You want to talk to Paul if you want to talk about that path."

I looked round the group of kids, who were openly backing away from us. The boy pointed further up the hill, to where a slightly younger lad was just climbing onto a brand new toboggan.

"Oi, Paul!" he shouted. "This lady wants to talk to you!"

Paul swooped down the road on his sled, and came to a halt in a spray of snow. He looked at me, puzzled.

"Tell her about that time we was playing football," the other boy prompted.

"What d'you mean?" asked Paul, "What time?"

"When the ball went down that path."

Realisation dawned on Paul, and the shadow that formed behind his eyes was alarming to witness. He swallowed hard, looked between the other boy and myself as if asking to be excused an unpleasant task.

"We were playing football…"

"I already said that, didn't I?" said the other. I suppressed a desire to kick him in the ankle.

"Yeah. Right. So I was in goal. Tony took a shot and it hit the lamppost and went off down the path. Now, I didn't think I should have had to go get it because he was the one who kicked it, but he said because it was his ball he didn't have to. So in the end I did."

There was an uncomfortable silence, until both I and the older boy said "Go on," at the same time.

"Well, as soon as I started walking down the path it got really cold," Paul said.

"When was this?" I interrupted. "What time of year?"

"Last summer holidays. So it was so cold I was even shivering. I could see the ball lying there in the middle of the path, but it seemed like a really long way away? Do you know what I mean?"

I nodded.

"I was walking towards it, but I never seemed to get any closer. And I felt really strange. Like, uncomfortable."

He paused and swallowed hard.

"Frightened."

Paul took a visible effort to compose himself, and continued.

"I think I would rather have done anything else than go and get that ball. I shouted for someone to come and help me…"

"We never heard nothing," said the other boy, quickly, almost guiltily.

"So in the end I finally got to the ball, and picked it up. But there were, like, whispers in my ears. Close. And as if people were blowing on the back of my neck."

I tried to look as sympathetic as I could. What I had just experienced on the path seemed to pale in comparison.

"And when I started walking back it was worse."

"When he came out it was nearly an hour later," interrupted the other boy.

I was astounded.

"You didn't go to look for him?' I asked, my opinion probably all too clear in my tone of voice.

"We figured the ball had rolled all the way down the hill and he'd met someone else down Castle Lane," said the older boy, hurriedly. But the explanation didn't ring true, and he knew it.

"So that's what happened," said Paul, keen to bring the conversation to a close.

"And when he got back," said the older boy. "His shoulders…"

"Steve, no…" said Paul, pleading.

"His shoulders was all covered in scratches."

"Steve!" said Paul, "You promised you'd never say anything…"

"Scratches?" I asked. "Like thorns, brambles?"

"No, like if a cat scratched you. Only bigger."

"Okay," I said. I had a thousand and one questions, but I didn't want to press Paul any further. "So this was last summer?" I asked Steve.

"Yeah, not long after we moved in."

"Was the path there? When you moved in, I mean?'

Paul and Steve exchanged glances. I got the impression that they'd talked about this before, but had not been believed.

"It wasn't there to start with," said Steve.

"But then it was," added Paul.

"Have you ever seen anyone using the path?" I asked.

They both shook their heads.

"Not at all? Not your parents, coming back from work or the shops?"

"No. Everybody uses the proper path if they have to walk down to Castle Lane."

"We drive everywhere," said Steve. "My dad's got a new Sierra."

I thanked them and walked back down to the curve in the road, and then down the tarmac footpath towards Castle Lane. It was clean and free of ice and snow, running between tall wooden fences, descending at a gentle gradient interspersed by a couple of flights of steps with cold steel railings. The other end of the desire path was harder to spot when I reached Castle Lane: a smaller gap between two trees. It seemed to be just as heavily trafficked as the end up on the new estate, all undergrowth worn away, the ground so compacted that the roots of the enclosing beech trees were like bones pushing through skin. As I stood there, peering into the gloom but with absolutely no desire to step on to the path, a middle-aged man approached along Castle Lane, leading a small terrier on a lead. I stood back to give them room, even wondering if the man and his dog would take the path, but we bumped into each other. The terrier was violently pulling his master away from the gap between the trees, and would have been in the road if he had not been on a lead.

. . .

I was now convinced that there was something deeply wrong about the desire path, and I felt certain that the problem was intangible, uncanny. Nobody was ever seen to use the path, nobody would admit to ever having used it, but it seemed as if dozens of pairs of feet trod it every day. I decided that the path needed to be closed off, somehow, but despite my neighbours' assumptions, my connections with the City Council were far too tenuous for me to be able to suggest this without significantly more evidence.

As soon as the Christmas and New Year holidays were over I started researching in the archives and the cathedral library. The proximity of the hill fort was suggestive: perhaps there had been an ancient trackway on the site, and the building of the new estate had "blocked" it? It made sense, but nothing I read covered a similar situation. Paths just did not appear, or reappear, even in paranormal circumstances. To put it simply, you might possibly see a ghostly legion marching through your spanking new living room, but you wouldn't be likely to discover a Roman road suddenly appearing in your rose bed. As I continued my research with little to show for it, the disturbing realisation that I would have to return – and walk the entire length of the path myself – grew in my mind.

∾

I decided to ask my old schoolfriend Claire Bessemer to come with me. I'm sure you all know Claire, and have heard that her role as "Environmental Protection Officer" for Barchester is about a lot more than simple fly-tipping or antisocial graffiti. At that point she was still apprenticed to her father, but she was the nearest thing to an expert in such matters I knew personally.

A week or so later, she met me at my house and we had a couple of stiff drinks to "keep out the cold" – really to bolster our courage. Then we walked down to Hillside Avenue and the top of the path.

It was a cold grey day, with a gusty easterly wind sending low black clouds scudding, seemingly just brushing the top of the hill fort.

As we arrived, Claire paused, as if sniffing the air.

"Hmmm…" was all she said. Then she reached into the old army surplus haversack she was using as a handbag and handed me a necklace of braided silver cord.

"Put this on. It might help," she said. I was puzzled, but slipped the circle of silver over my head and around my neck. It was cold against my skin, but felt oddly comforting.

I fought the instinct to hold Claire's hand as we stepped onto the path.

Just as on the previous occasion it instantly became a lot colder and silence fell. Even though the blustery winds were scattering leaves under the trees to both sides of the path, they made no sound. We both hunched against the cold and pressed on. The path was frozen under our boots, but completely clear of leaves or the frosty remnants of snow that still persisted under the trees. Our breath clouded in the air.

The path wound downhill, twisting and turning apparently at random. Although the trees were bare, it seemed unnaturally dark.

We had reached what must surely have been the halfway point between Hillside Avenue and Castle Lane, though the snaky path made judging distances difficult. We could no longer see the entrance behind us, nor yet see the bottom end of the track.

The silence was broken.

It began as a hissing sound, what might have been the wind blowing through the branches, but it soon resolved into a whispering voice.

We both paused and looked around. I felt a chill as I remembered the earlier rumours about a flasher. Was that the solution to the mystery after all?

There was nobody to be seen.

And then more voices joined in.

The whispering was too quiet to be deciphered, though it was rhythmical, like a chorus or a chant. At times it seemed to be coming from under the trees to ether side, at others it was almost as if the speaker was standing right beside us, whispering in our ears.

And then a sharper, more percussive noise, a pattering, like the sound of dry leaves being skittered on the wind, but too regular. The sound grew in volume, and was multiplied.

Footsteps.

Claire and I looked at each other.

Running footsteps. Approaching us along the path. We couldn't tell from which direction.

We looked behind us, and then as far down the hill as we could see, but there was nothing. Yet the footsteps grew closer.

Closer.

And then they were on top of us.

I was nearly knocked off my feet as an unseen body barged past me. I could feel the heat of panting breath, and a gamey, sweaty odour of an unwashed body and damp clothing; wool and half-cured animal skin. Just as I regained my balance, another body pushed me aside, coming from the opposite direction. I heard the hiss of words in a foreign tongue, not one I recognised, though it sounded exotic and harsh. Ancient.

The silver necklace, which had been uncomfortably cold against my neck, started to feel warm.

I looked across to Claire. She too was being buffeted by unseen runners. The sound of their voices grew louder. Angry, threatening.

We started to run ourselves. It was pure instinct.

Panic. I felt I had never really understood the term before. It was visceral, primal.

The twisting path conspired against us, the footing treacherous, icy and criss-crossed by snaking roots. Branches seemed to grab at our hair as we passed, or to whip in our faces. Both of us stumbled. When Claire fell it was all I could do to stop and turn to help her back to her feet. The path seemed impossibly long, twisting back on itself. It was as if the thin strip of woodland had become a huge ancient forest.

My head was jerked back as if my hair was being pulled. I reached up, thinking I had snagged it on a branch.

But my fingers closed on an ice-cold hand, gripping tight.

I pinched the chill flesh as hard as I could and jerked my head forward. I felt a small clump of hair being torn out by the roots, but ignored the pain.

We ran faster, and the unseen ran alongside us, hounding, harrying. We were barged into and tripped. Sharp fingers pinched our arms and plate-sized palms pushed us between the shoulder blades. The contemptuous hissing syllables spat in our ears.

I believe I was close to hysteria, feeling a scream building in my chest. Then suddenly it was over. We crashed out of the footpath onto Castle Lane, sliding across the icy pavement, almost into the road.

. . .

I reached up to the back of my head and felt a raw spot the size of a 5p piece where my hair had been pulled out. Claire's face was badly scratched. One knee of her jeans torn when she had fallen.

Panting, she looked at her watch.

"How long do you think we were in there?" she asked, after a moment.

"Five minutes?" I replied.

She held up her watch. It had been almost an hour.

Together we got the desire path, in fact that whole patch of woodland, fenced off. I believe the cover story was that the path was unsafe, and the City Council might find itself facing an expensive damages case if anyone were injured on it. Tall close-set fences appeared over a weekend, though apparently there were complaints from the builders, who said they didn't like working under the trees.

If you looked through a knot-hole in the right place, you could see the path. Still clear. Still apparently in constant use.

There is a sequel, which perhaps goes some way towards explaining the mystery. Draw your own conclusions.

Almost a decade later the police raided the home

of one of the builders who'd worked on the Hillside estate. They were looking for Class A drugs, but in addition found something quite different.

It was a small block of carved sandstone, which was later identified as Roman, something like an altar or tombstone, but differing from either in several notable details. The builder had uncovered it while digging the foundations of one of the new houses, and had carried it off. He had intended to sell it for drug money but found that, unlike his usual loot of car stereos or lawn mowers, no-one was interested in buying it.

The inscription was worn, and cryptic, but some experts claimed that it could be translated as "To Quieten the Angry Multitude".

I understand that Claire soon got hold of it, and secretly re-buried it at the Castle Lane end of the footpath amid a short arcane ceremony.

If one were to look over those tall fences today, there would be no sign that the path had ever existed.

STILL WATERS

GREG'S STORY

STILL WATERS

I t was the first meeting of the Talespinners since the New Year. Outside, brisk northerly gusts blew swirls of snow against the tiny old windows of The Old Inn and occasional high-pitched draughts found their way in around the frames. At the large round table beside the inglenook fireplace, however, all was warm and cosy.

Once the latest round of drinks had been distributed, the four other members of the group waited for Greg, the writer, to tell his story. As was appropriate for his profession, he had typed it out, and shuffled a few pages of printed A4 on the table in front of him.

"This happened a couple of years ago, in weather that was the absolute opposite of today's. I will not go into details regarding the location. I know how curious some of you can be, and I would not want to be responsible for what might happen if you went to try and find the place."

I had first found the pool during the green heat of July, when the woods had been loud with the electric buzz of insects and the calls of unseen birds. It was the hottest day of a hot year, and I had wandered from my usual route across the downs into the valley in the hope of finding some running water to cool myself. After a period of walking through thick woodland the trees began to thin and I soon found myself in an open glade, bare of vegetation and carpeted with fallen leaves.

That was my first sight of the pool. It was circular and maybe fifteen feet across, enclosed within a couple of courses of weathered stone blocks. Surrounded entirely by towering trees, it seemed like a sanctuary deep in the woods, the kind of place where mythic nymphs might have been caught bathing by hapless mortals. As this charming thought flitted through my mind, however, a surprisingly chill breeze had blown up from nowhere, corrugating the black surface of the pool, and I felt a frisson of dread crawl up my spine.

I walked towards the dark water, feeling strangely disturbed. The pool, black as a bath of Indian ink, seemed profound, uncomfortably deep. Standing near the edge and leaning forward I could discern pebbles and dead leaves on the bed of the pool within a few inches of the containing wall, but beyond that the water darkened as it deepened and soon seemed impenetrable. There were no weeds nor any other sign of life in the water, not even any insects hovering over the surface. The pool seemed not so much stagnant as completely unnatural – as though it was filled with oil or some other noxious liquid. I was almost afraid it would smell rank, but although I sniffed hard I could detect no odour whatsoever.

The chill breeze ruffled the water once again and I became aware of how cold it had become. The sultry heat of summer might as well have been months past and although I was only a few yards away from the trees I could hear neither insects nor birds. I looked back over my shoulder at the trees, thick as a garden hedge, through which I has so recently made my way, and felt completely isolated.

There was a noise from the pool – not so much a splash, more like the settling of liquid, like a body easing into a warm bath. I swung my head around to look but saw nothing but slow ripples progressing from a point near the centre of the pool. They broke against the rim like lazy waves and died before they could rebound. Something large had obviously moved deep in the water. Almost unconsciously I took a step back from the edge.

I was colder than the chill breeze would account for, and felt a shivering nervousness wash over me, like one of those irrational childhood panics. In the space of a few seconds the aspect of the pool had changed from a charming idyll to something oddly sinister. I found myself backing slowly away from the black water, not knowing why I was disturbed, but happier to put some distance between myself and it. I stumbled against a fallen branch, nearly losing my footing, and glanced down at my feet for a moment. When I looked back up at the pool the water was settling again, the ripples moving across the surface like snakes slithering through grass. Still backing away I watched as one of the wavelets broke over the stone coping, splashing a cupful of inky liquid on the smooth surface of the old stone. The spilt water coalesced, then seemed to move of its own accord, sending out a searching tendril across the stone. I backed into one of the willow trees with a thump that almost winded me, then turned on my heels and hurried away.

I returned to the pool a few days later, although I had intended to stay well away from it. I had found it strangely disturbing, and the sense of panic was uncomfortably clear in my memory. Yet, when I next found myself in the same area of the woods, I almost instinctively sought it out.

This time I looked out for it as I approached through the trees, and was surprised to find that it remained out of sight until I was almost on top of it. I stepped into the clearing and heard the water settle, almost in welcome. The pool was just as I remembered, trapped in its bubble of wintry atmosphere, dark, and mysterious.

It still disturbed me, but I forced myself to approach its inky eye. What could I possibly have to fear? Shivering despite the blazing sunshine, I lowered myself to sit on the stone coping. The water moved in a long slow swell like an ocean wave.

I had not bothered to examine the construction of the pool before, but as I sat there I was surprised to see that the fabric of the containing wall seemed to be blocks of dressed granite – certainly not a local material. The stones were all expertly laid so that there was hardly more than a paper-thin gap between them. It was work of some expertise and, I assumed, expense.

As I ran my fingers over the smooth stone, wondering how long ago the craftsmen had constructed this impeccable piece of work, and on whose orders, I found my fingertips trembling over an imperfection in the otherwise perfect block. I looked closer, and found a set of carved initials. They were cut deep and with some skill and read "G. T. 1846 AD". So the pool was at least that old. Nearby I noticed other initials. Intrigued, I started copying them down on the back of an envelope I found in my jacket pocket. I made an entire circuit of the pool in my search. The most recent graffiti was a few years old, the oldest apparently dating from 1537, if that was to be believed.

I was examining that last inscription when the pool gave another sigh – no splash, just the sonorous displacement of water. I looked up. A wavelet broke, soundlessly, on the coping beside me and the inky liquid trickled – almost crawled - across the granite towards me. I jolted backwards and stood straight. As I caught my breath the water ran quietly back into the pool.

Sitting down again I noticed another inscription, worn away by the passage of time and now very indistinct, though originally it had been carved deeper, and in larger letters, than any of the others. I examined it for some minutes, running my fingers over the blurred lettering and even crouching to look at it from an oblique angle, hoping to throw it into clearer relief. In the end I only managed to decipher –AV– AQV– I attempted to translate this, like a half completed crossword answer, into a recognisable name, but got nowhere. Then it occurred to me that it might possibly be Latin. Having made that jump of logic it did not take me long to think of CAVE AQVA, which I took to mean Beware of the Water – maybe there was a further inscription meaning DEEP or something of that sort. CAVE AQVA PROFVNDA perhaps? My grammar school had sought to emulate public schools in many ways, one of which was compulsory Latin for the first three years, but that had been decades ago. I looked again and felt with my fingertips, but any additional lettering had long since worn away. Presumably this had been carved as a warning against the perils of bathing in the pool – but could it really date back to Roman times, or at least to times when literacy meant literacy in Latin? Staring into the inky water I shivered. That it was deep enough to warrant such a warning was evident, but I could not imagine any passer-by, however travel-worn, wanting to enter the unappealing depths. The pool seemed too small to swim in anyway; more like a large cistern to provide drinking facilities for man and beast. Though again the water looked far from appetising.

The sun was getting low in the west, flinging the long shadows of the surrounding trees across the wall of the pool, and I decided it was time to leave.

I had taken just a few steps when I heard the water heave and settle once again, and looked back to see waves – larger than the ripples I had seen before – radiate with stately grace across the diameter of the pool, to break sluggishly against the enclosing stones. There was obviously something very large living in the water. I knew that carp could attain prodigious size in their long lives, though I doubted there was room for the pool to support more than a couple. I moved nearer again, wondering if I could catch a glimpse of the leviathan fish that was moving in the darkness. As I watched, the surface of the water gathered and heaved up – slowly, as if it denser than normal – then collapsed again, sending larger waves still progressing towards the containing wall.

Once again these waves broke, and a large

amount of the black water – almost a saucepan full – splashed on top of the granite blocks. A nervous thought briefly crossed my mind: perhaps the Latin inscription had not been about the dangers of bathing, but a warning against something living in the water. But that was patently ridiculous. I stepped a little closer.

As I thought I had seen once before, the spilled liquid seemed to coalesce, forming a miniature pool, inky black like its parent. Then, as I watched, a tendril of water broke away, running across the marble towards me. This gave me a jolt like a small electric shock, and I laughed nervously. The water stopped moving, but did not run back into the pool.

There was another resonant displacement of the water and another litre or so was splashed onto the stone coping.

Before my eyes this second, larger, puddle gathered itself together and then *slithered* over the worn marble until it met and united with the first. And then the tendril began to move again, its tip moving fast, confidently… towards me.

Have you ever watched an amoeba under a microscope? That was how it seemed to me. I began stepping backwards. My belly was full of ice and I wanted to be as far from the pool as possible, yet I could not tear my eyes away from the bizarre spectacle I was witness to. Each time the tendril reached its limit, another convulsion would sweep the pool, depositing more water on the marble to feed the filament and push it further still.

The seeking tip of liquid reached the edge of the stone and rolled over – *slowly* – like syrup, flowing smoothly down onto the dusty ground, where it settled, collecting itself.

The pool heaved again, and more liquid fed the strangely mobile tendril. It struck out again, the tip moving from side to side, like a dog searching out a scent. I wanted to turn and run, but was transfixed.

CAVE AQVA.

Each time the pool settled, liquid was deposited on other points around the marble, each feeding a similarly mobile puddle.

Other tendrils had struck out from the source, manoeuvred, positioned themselves.

It was as if the water – or whatever the liquid was – had not only a life of its own, but awareness, intelligence, too.

Tendrils were advancing on me from three sides.

CAVE AQVA.

Not an injunction against bathing.

Nor a caution about something that lived *in* the pool.

But a warning against the pool itself…

The first tendril touched my foot. It felt heavy, thick. It broke the spell. I turned and ran headlong.

I have never returned to those woods since.

AFTERWORD

The initial idea which has since grown into "Wyrd Barchester" came from the juxtaposition of my life-long love of supernatural stories and tales of the uncanny, and a conversation late one evening in one of Salisbury's many old and ghost-ridden pubs (a time and place where such revelations are not uncommon). The subject under discussion was the city's location on the confluence of five rivers, and the mystic implications of this. That started me thinking about other unusual aspects of Salisbury: its place in the centre of a unique and ancient ritual landscape, the associated web of ley lines which are said to converge there, and the odd proximity of military bases and secret government establishments to the ancient monuments. All of which led me to the conclusion that if Salisbury wasn't a weird, paranormal, locus then it ought to be...

I chose to fictionalise Salisbury under the name of

Barchester as a nod to literary precedent (both Anthony Trollope and M.R. James based their "Barchesters" in the most part on Salisbury) but also to allow me a little artistic licence when it came to geography.

ABOUT THE AUTHOR

Jim Radley was born in Gillingham, Kent and now lives in Salisbury, Wiltshire.

facebook.com/wyrdbarchester

ALSO BY JIM RADLEY

Printed in Great Britain
by Amazon